The Inner Beauty

The Inner Beauty

by Maurice Maeterlinck

Copyright © 9/2/2015
Jefferson Publication

ISBN-13: 978-1517174873

Printed in the United States of America

Contents

THE INNER BEAUTY

Nothing in the whole world is so athirst for beauty as the soul, nor is there anything to which beauty clings so readily.

There is nothing in the world capable of such spontaneous uplifting, of such speedy ennoblement; nothing that offers more scrupulous obedience to the pure and noble commands it receives.

There is nothing in the world that yields deeper submission to the empire of a thought that is loftier than other thoughts. And on this earth of ours there are but few souls that can withstand the dominion of the soul that has suffered itself to become beautiful.

In all truth might it be said that beauty is the unique aliment of our soul, for in all places does it search for beauty, and it perishes not of hunger even in the most degraded of lives. For indeed nothing of beauty can pass by and be altogether unperceived. Perhaps does it never pass by save only in our unconsciousness, but its action is no less puissant in gloom of night than by light of day; the joy it procures may be less tangible, but other difference there is none.

Look at the most ordinary of men, at a time when a little beauty has contrived to steal into their darkness. They have come together, it matters not where, and for no special reason; but no sooner are they assembled than their very first thought would seem to be to close the great doors of life. Yet has each one of them, when alone, more than once lived in accord with his soul. He has loved

3

perhaps, of a surety he has suffered. Inevitably must he, too, have heard the sounds that come from the distant country of Splendor and Terror, and many an evening has he bowed down in silence before laws that are deeper than the sea. And yet when these men are assembled it is with the basest of things that they love to debauch themselves. They have a strange indescribable fear of beauty, and as their number increases so does this fear become greater, resembling indeed their dread of silence or of a verity that is too pure. And so true is this that, were one of them to have done something heroic in the course of the day, he would ascribe wretched motives to his conduct, thereby endeavoring to find excuses for it, and these motives would lie readily to his hand in that lower region where he and his fellows were assembled.

And yet listen: a proud and lofty word has been spoken, a word that has in a measure undammed the springs of life. For one instant has a soul dared to reveal itself, even such as it is in love and sorrow, such as it is in face of death and in the solitude that dwells around the stars of night. Disquiet prevails, on some faces there is astonishment, others smile. But have you never felt at moments such as those how unanimous is the fervor wherewith every soul admires, and how unspeakably even the very feeblest, from the remotest depths of its dungeon, approves the word it has recognized as akin to itself? For they have all suddenly sprung to life again in the primitive and normal atmosphere that is their own; and could you but hearken with angels' ears, I doubt not but you would hear mightiest applause in that kingdom of amazing radiance wherein the souls do dwell.

Do you not think that even the most timid of them would take courage unto themselves were but similar words to be spoken every evening? Do you not think that men would live purer lives? And yet though the word come not again, still will something momentous have happened, that must leave still more momentous trace behind. Every evening will its sisters recognize the soul that pronounced the word, and henceforth, be the conversation never so trivial, its mere presence will, I know not how, add thereto something of majesty. Whatever else betide, there has been a change that we cannot determine. No longer will such absolute

4

power be vested in the baser side of things, and henceforth, even the most terror-stricken of souls will know that there is somewhere a place of refuge....

Certain it is that the natural and primitive relationship of soul to soul is a relationship of beauty. For beauty is the only language of our soul; none other is known to it. It has no other life, it can produce nothing else, in nothing else can it take interest. And therefore it is that the most oppressed, nay, the most degraded of souls—if it may truly be said that a soul can be degraded—immediately hail with acclamation every thought, every word or deed, that is great and beautiful.

Beauty is the only element wherewith the soul is organically connected, and it has no other standard of judgment. This is brought home to us at every moment of our life, and is no less evident to the man by whom beauty may more than once have been denied than to him who is ever seeking it in his heart. Should a day come when you stand in profoundest need of another's sympathy, would you go to him who was wont to greet the passage of beauty with a sneering smile? Would you go to him whose shake of the head had sullied a generous action or a mere impulse that was pure? Even though perhaps you had been of those who commended him, you would none the less, when it was truth that knocked at your door, turn to the man who had known how to prostrate himself and love. In its very depths had your soul passed its judgment, and it is the silent and unerring judgment that will rise to the surface, after thirty years perhaps, and send you towards a sister who shall be more truly you than you are yourself, for that she has been nearer to beauty.... There needs but so little to encourage beauty in our soul; so little to awaken the slumbering angels; or perhaps is there no need of awakening—it is enough that we lull them not to sleep.

It requires more effort to fall, perhaps, than to rise.

Can we, without putting constraint upon ourselves, confine our thoughts to everyday things at times when the sea stretches before us, and we are face to face with the night? And what soul is there but knows that it is ever confronting the sea, ever in presence of an eternal night?

Did we but dread beauty less it would come about that nought else in life would be visible; for in reality it is beauty that underlies everything, it is beauty alone that exists. There is no soul but is conscious of this, none that is not in readiness; but where are those that hide not their beauty? And yet must one of them "begin." Why not dare to be the one to "begin." The others are all watching eagerly around us like little children in front of a marvelous place. They press upon the threshold, whispering to each other and peering through every crevice, but there is not one who dares put his shoulder to the door. They are all waiting for some grown-up person to come and fling it open. But hardly ever does such a one pass by.

And yet what is needed to become the grown-up person for whom they lie in wait? So little! The soul is not exacting. A thought that is almost beautiful—a thought that you speak not, but that you cherish within you at this moment, will irradiate you as though you were a transparent vase. They will see it and their greeting to you will be very different than had you been meditating how best to deceive your brother.

We are surprised when certain men tell us that they have never come across real ugliness, that they cannot conceive that a soul can be base.

Yet need there be no cause for surprise. These men had "begun." They themselves had been the first to be beautiful, and had therefore attracted all the beauty that passed by, as a lighthouse attracts the vessels from the four corners of the horizon. But there are those who complain of women, for instance, never dreaming that, the first time a man meets a woman, a single word or thought that denies the beautiful or profound will be enough to poison for ever his existence in her soul. "For my part," said a sage to me one day, "I have never come across a single woman who did not bring to me something that was great." He was great himself first of all; therein lay his secret.

There is one thing only that the soul can never forgive; it is to have been compelled to behold, or share, or pass close to an ugly action, word, or thought. It cannot forgive, for forgiveness here were but the denial of itself.

And yet with the generality of men, ingenuity, strength and skill do but imply that the soul must first of all be banished from their life, and that every impulse that lies too deep must be carefully brushed aside. Even in love do they act thus, and therefore, it is that the woman, who is so much nearer the truth, can scarcely ever live a moment of the true life with them. It is as though men dreaded the contact of their soul, and were anxious to keep its beauty at immeasurable distance. Whereas, on the contrary, we should endeavor to move in advance of ourselves.

If at this moment you think or say something that is too beautiful to be true in you—if you have but endeavored to think or say it to-day, on the morrow it will be true. We must try to be more beautiful than ourselves; we shall never distance our soul.

We can never err when it is question of silent or hidden beauty. Besides, so long as the spring within us be limpid, it matters but little whether error there be or not. But do any of us ever dream of making the slightest unseen effort? And yet in the domain where we are everything is effective, for that everything is waiting.

All the doors are unlocked, we have but to push them open, and the palace is full of manacled queens.

A single word will very often suffice to clear the mountain of refuse.

Why not have the courage to meet a base question with a noble answer? Do you imagine it would pass quite unnoticed or merely arouse surprise? Do you not think it would be more akin to the discourse that would naturally be held between two souls? We know not where it may give encouragement, where freedom. Even he who rejects your word will, in spite of himself, have taken a step towards the beauty that is within him.

Nothing of beauty dies without having purified something, nor can aught of beauty be lost. Let us not be afraid of sowing it along the road. It may remain there for weeks or years, but like the diamond it cannot dissolve, and finally there will pass by some one whom its glitter will attract; he will pick it up and go his way, rejoicing. Then why keep back a lofty, beautiful word, for that you doubt whether others will understand? An instant of higher goodness was impending over you; why hinder its coming, even though you believe not that those about you will profit thereby? What if you are among men of the valley, is that sufficient reason for checking the instinctive movement of your soul towards the mountain peaks? Does darkness rob deep feeling of its power?

Have the blind nought but their eyes wherewith to distinguish those who love them from those who love them not? Can the beauty not exist that is not understood, and is there not in every man something that does understand—in regions far beyond what he seems to understand, far beyond, too, what he believes he understands? "Even to the very wretchedest of all," said to me one day the loftiest minded creature it has ever been my happiness to know, "even to the very wretchedest of all I never have the courage to say anything in reply that is ugly or mediocre." I have for a long time followed that man's life, and have seen the inexplicable power he exercised over the most obscure, the most unapproachable, the blindest, even the most rebellious of souls. For no tongue can tell the power of a soul that strives to live in an atmosphere of beauty, and is actively beautiful in itself. And indeed is it not the quality of this activity that renders life either miserable or divine?

If we could but probe to the root of things it might well be discovered that it is by the strength of some souls that are beautiful that others are sustained in life.

Is it not the idea we each form of certain chosen ones that constitutes the only living, effective morality? But in this idea how much is there of the soul that is chosen, how much of him who chooses?

Do not these things blend very mysteriously, and does not this ideal morality lie infinitely deeper than the morality of the most beautiful books? A far-reaching influence exists therein whose limits it is indeed difficult to define, and a fountain of strength whereat we all of us drink many times a day. Would not any weakness in one of those creatures whom you thought perfect, and loved in the region of beauty, at once lessen your confidence in the universal greatness of things, and would your admiration for them suffer?

And again, I doubt whether anything in the world can beautify a soul more spontaneously, more naturally, than the knowledge that somewhere in its neighborhood there exists a pure and noble being whom it can unreservedly love. When the soul has veritably drawn near to such a being, beauty is no longer a lovely, lifeless thing, that one exhibits to the stranger, for it suddenly takes unto itself an imperious existence, and its activity becomes so natural as to be henceforth irresistible. Wherefore you will do well to think it over, for none are alone, and those who are good must watch.

Plotinus, in the eighth book of the fifth "Ennead," after speaking of the beauty that is "intelligible"—*i. e.* divine—concludes thus: "As regards ourselves, we are beautiful when we belong to ourselves, and ugly when we lower ourselves to our inferior nature. Also are we beautiful when we know such knowledge." Bear it in mind, however, that here we are on the mountains, where not to know oneself means far more than mere ignorance of what takes place within us at moments of jealousy or love, fear or envy, happiness or unhappiness. Here not to know oneself means to be unconscious of all the divine that throbs in man.

As we wander from the gods within us so does ugliness enwrap us; as we discover them, so do we become more beautiful. But it is only by revealing the divine that is in us that we may discover the divine in others.

Needs must one god beckon to another, and no signal is so imperceptible but they will every one of them respond. It cannot be said too often that, be the crevice never so small, it will yet suffice for all the waters of heaven to pour into our soul.

Every cup is stretched out to the unknown spring, and we are in a region where none think of aught but beauty.

If we could ask of an angel what it is that our souls do in the shadow, I believe the angel would answer, after having looked for many years perhaps, and seen far more than the things the soul seems to do in the eyes of men, "They transform into beauty all the little things that are given to them." Ah! we must admit that the human soul is possessed of singular courage! Resignedly does it labor, its whole life long, in the darkness whither most of us relegate it, where it is spoken to by none. There, never complaining, does it do all that in its power lies, striving to tear from out the pebbles we fling to it the nucleus of eternal light that peradventure they contain. And in the midst of its work it is ever lying in wait for the moment when it may show, to a sister who is more tenderly cared for, or who chances to be nearer, the treasures it has so toilfully amassed.

But thousands of existences there are that no sister visits; thousands of existences wherein life has infused such timidity into the soul that it departs without saying a word, without even once having been able to deck itself with the humblest jewels of its humble crown....

And yet, in spite of all, does it watch over everything from out its invisible heaven. It warns and loves, it admires, attracts, repels. At every fresh event does it rise to the surface, where it lingers till it be thrust down again, being looked upon as wearisome and insane. It wanders to and fro, like Cassandra at the gates of the Atrides. It is ever giving utterance to words of shadowy truth, but there are none to listen. When we raise our eyes it yearns for a ray of sun or star, that it may weave into a thought, or, haply, an impulse, which shall be unconscious and very pure. And if our eyes bring it nothing, still will it know how to turn its pitiful disillusion into something ineffable, that it will conceal even till its death.

When we love, how eagerly does it drink in the light from behind the closed door—keen with expectation, it yet wastes not a minute, and the light that steals through the apertures becomes beauty and truth to the soul. But if the door open not (and how many lives are there wherein it does open?) it will go back into its prison, and its regret will perhaps be a loftier verity that shall never be seen, for we are now in the region of transformations whereof none may speak; and though nothing born this side of the door can be lost, yet does it never mingle with our life....

I said just now that the soul changed into beauty the little things we gave to it. It would even seem, the more we think of it, that the soul has no other reason for existence, and that all its activity is consumed in amassing, at the depths of us, a treasure of indescribable beauty. Might not everything naturally turn into beauty, were we not unceasingly interrupting the arduous labors of our soul? Does not evil itself become precious so soon as it has gathered therefrom the deep lying diamond of repentance? The acts of injustice whereof you have been guilty, the tears you have caused to flow, will not these end too by becoming so much radiance and love in your soul? Have you ever cast your eyes into this kingdom of purifying flame that is within you?

Perhaps a great wrong may have been done you to-day, the act itself being mean and disheartening, the mode of action of the basest, and ugliness wrapped you round as your tears fell. But let some years elapse, then give one look into your soul, and tell me whether, beneath the recollection of that act, you see not something that is already purer than thought; an indescribable, unnameable force that has nought in common with the forces of this world; a mysterious inexhaustible spring of the other life, whereat you may drink for the rest of your days.

And yet will you have rendered no assistance to the untiring queen; other thoughts will have filled your mind, and it will be without your knowledge that the act will have been purified in the silence of your being, and will have flown into the precious waters that lie in the great reservoir of truth and beauty, which, unlike the shallower reservoir of true or beautiful thoughts, has an ever unruffled surface, and remains for all time out of reach of the breath of life.

Emerson tells us that there is not an act or event in our life but, sooner or later, casts off its outer shell, and bewilders us by its sudden flights from the very depths of us, on high into the empyrean. And this is true to a far greater extent than Emerson had foreseen, for the further we advance in these regions, the diviner are the spheres we discover.

We can form no adequate conception of what this silent activity of the souls that surround us may really mean. Perhaps you have spoken a pure word to one of your fellows by whom it has not been understood. You look upon it as lost and dismiss it from your mind. But one day, peradventure, the word comes up again extraordinarily transformed, and revealing the unexpected fruit it has borne in the darkness; then silence once more falls over all. But it matters not; we have learned that nothing can be lost in the soul, and that even to the very pettiest there come moments of splendor.

It is unmistakably borne home to us that even the unhappiest and the most destitute of men have at the depths of their being and in spite of themselves a treasure of beauty that they cannot despoil. They have but to acquire the habit of dipping into this treasurer. It suffices not that beauty should keep solitary festival in life; it has to become a festival of every day.

There needs no great effort to be admitted into the ranks of those "whose eyes no longer behold earth in flower and sky in glory in infinitesimal fragments, but indeed in sublime masses," and I speak here of flowers and sky that are purer and more lasting than those that we behold.

Thousands of channels there are through which the beauty of our soul may sail even unto our thoughts. Above all is there the wonderful, central channel of love.

Is it not in love that are found the purest elements of beauty that we can offer to the soul?

Some there are who do thus in beauty love each other. And to love thus means that, little by little, the sense of ugliness is lost; that one's eyes are closed to all the littlenesses of life, to all but the freshness and virginity of the very humblest of souls. Loving thus, we have no longer even the need to forgive. Loving thus, we can no longer have anything to conceal, for that the ever-present soul transforms all things into beauty. It is to behold evil in so far only as it purifies indulgence, and teaches us no longer to confound the sinner with his sin. Loving thus do we raise on high within ourselves all those about us who have attained an eminence where failure has become impossible; heights whence a paltry action has so far to fall that, touching earth, it is compelled to yield up its diamond soul.

It is to transform, though all unconsciously, the feeblest intention that hovers about us into illimitable movement. It is to summon all that is beautiful in earth, heaven or soul, to the banquet of love.

Loving thus, we do indeed exist before our fellows as we exist before God. It means that the least gesture will call forth the presence of the soul with all its treasure. No longer is there need of death, disaster or tears for that the soul shall appear; a smile suffices.

Loving thus, we perceive truth in happiness as profoundly as some of the heroes perceived it in the radiance of greatest sorrow. It means that the beauty that turns into love is undistinguishable from the love that turns into beauty. It means to be able no longer to tell where the ray of a star leaves off and the kiss of an ordinary thought begins. It means to have come so near to God that the angels possess us.

13

Loving thus, the same soul will have been so beautified by us all that it will become, little by little, the "unique angel" mentioned by Swedenborg. It means that each day will reveal to us a new beauty in that mysterious angel, and that we shall walk together in a goodness that shall ever become more and more living, loftier and loftier. For there exists also a lifeless beauty, made up of the past alone; but the veritable love renders the past useless, and its approach creates a boundless future of goodness, without disaster and without tears.

To love thus is but to free one's soul, and to become as beautiful as the soul thus freed. "If, in the emotion that this spectacle cannot fail to awaken in thee," says the great Plotinus, when dealing with kindred matters—and of all the intellects known to me that of Plotinus draws the nearest to the divine—"If in the emotion that this spectacle cannot fail to awaken in thee, thou proclaimest not that it is beautiful; and if, plunging thine eyes into thyself, thou dost not then feel the charm of beauty, it is in vain that, thy disposition being such, thou shouldst seek the intelligible beauty; for thou wouldst seek it only with that which is ugly and impure. Therefore it is that the discourse we hold here is not addressed to all men. But if thou hast recognized beauty within thyself, see that thou rise to the recollection of the intelligible beauty."

THE INVISIBLE GOODNESS

It is a thing, said to me one evening the sage I had chanced to meet by the sea shore, whereon the waves were breaking almost noiselessly—it is a thing that we scarcely notice, that none seem to take into account, and yet do I conceive it to be one of the forces that safeguard mankind. In a thousand diverse ways do the gods from whom we spring reveal themselves within us, but it may well be that this unnoticed secret goodness, to which sufficiently direct allusion has never yet been made, is the purest token of their eternal life. Whence it comes we know not. It is there in its simplicity, smiling on the threshold of our soul; and those in whom its smiles lies deepest, or shine forth most frequently, may make us suffer day and night and they will, yet shall it be beyond our power to cease to love them....

It is not of this world, and still are there few agitations of ours in which it takes not part. It cares not to reveal itself even in look or tear. Nay, it seeks concealment, for reasons one cannot divine. It is as though it were afraid to make use of its power. It knows that its most involuntary movement will cause immortal things to spring to life about it; and we are miserly with immortal things. Why are we so fearful lest we exhaust the heaven within us? We dare not act upon the whisper of the God who inspires us. We are afraid of everything that cannot be explained by word or gesture; and we shut our eyes to all that we do, ourselves notwithstanding, in the empire where explanations are vain!

Whence comes the timidity of the divine in man? For truly might it be said that the nearer a movement of our soul approaches the divine, so much the more scrupulously do we conceal it from the eyes of our brethren. Can it be that man is nothing but a frightened god? Or has the command been laid upon us that the superior powers must not be betrayed? Upon all that does not form part of this too visible world there rests the tender meekness of the little ailing girl, for whom her mother will not send when strangers come to the house.

And therefore it is that this secret goodness of ours has never yet passed through the silent portals of our soul. It lives within us like a prisoner forbidden to approach the barred window of her cell. But indeed, what matter though it do not approach? Enough that it be there. Hide as it may, let it but raise its head, move a link of its chain or open its hand, and the prison is illumined, the pressure of radiance from within bursts open the iron barrier, and then, suddenly, there yawns a gulf between words and beings, a gulf peopled with agitated angels; silence falls over all: the eyes turn away for a moment and two souls embrace tearfully on the threshold....

It is not a thing that comes from this earth of ours, and all descriptions can be of no avail. They who would understand must have, in themselves too, the same point of sensibility. If you have never in your life felt the power of your invisible goodness, go no further; it would be useless. But are there really any who have not felt this power, and have the worst of us never been invisibly good? I know not: of so many in this world does the aim seem to be the discouragement of the divine in their soul. And yet there needs but one instant of respite for the divine to spring up again, and even the wickedest are not incessantly on their guard; and hence doubtless has it arisen that so many of the wicked are good, unseen of all, whereas divers saints and sages are not invisibly good....

More than once have I been the cause of suffering, he went on, even as each being is the cause of suffering about him.

I have caused suffering because we are in a world where all is held together by invisible threads, in a world where none are alone, and where the gentlest gesture of love or kindliness may so often wound the innocence by our side!—

I have caused suffering, too, because there are times when the best and tenderest are impelled to seek I know not what part of themselves in the grief of others. For, indeed, there are seeds that only spring up in our soul beneath the rain of tears shed because of us, and none the less do these seeds produce good flowers and salutary fruit. What would you? It is no law of our making, and I know not whether I would dare to love the man who had made no one weep.

Frequently, indeed, will the greatest suffering be caused by those whose love is greatest, for a strange, timid, tender cruelty is most often the anxious sister of love. On all sides does love search for the proofs of love, and the first proofs—who is not prone to discover them in the tears of the beloved?

16

Even death could not suffice to reassure the lover who dared to give ear to the unreasoning claims of love; for to the intimate cruelty of love, the instant of death seems too brief; over beyond death there is yet room for a sea of doubts, and even in those who die together may disquiet still linger as they die. Long, slowly falling tears are needed here. Grief is love's first food, and every love that has not been fed on a little pure suffering must die like the babe that one had tried to nourish on the nourishment of a man. Will the love inspired by the woman who always brought the smile to your lips be quite the same as the love you feel for her who at times called forth your tears? Alas! needs must love weep, and often indeed is it at the very moment when the sobs burst forth that love's chains are forged and tempered for life....

Thus, he continued, I have caused suffering because I loved, and also have I caused suffering because I did not love—but how great was the difference in the two cases! In the one the slowly dropping tears of well-tried love seemed already to know, at the depths of them, that they were bedewing all that was ineffable in our united souls; in the other the poor tears knew that they were falling in solitude on a desert. But it is at those very moments when the soul is all ear—or, haply, all soul—that I have recognized the might of an invisible goodness that could offer to the wretched tears of an expiring love the divine illusions of a love on the eve of birth. Has there never come to you one of those sorrowful evenings when dejection lay heavy upon your unsmiling kisses, and it at length dawned upon your soul that it had been mistaken? With direst difficulty did your words ring forth in the cold air of the separation that was to be final; you were about to part for ever, and your almost lifeless hands were outstretched for the farewell of a departure that should know no return, when suddenly your soul made an imperceptible movement within itself. On that instant did the soul by the side of you awake on the summits of its being; something sprang to life in regions loftier far than the love of jaded lovers; and for all that the bodies might shrink asunder, henceforth would the souls never forget that for an instant they had beheld each other high above mountains they had never seen, and that for a second's space they had been good with a goodness they had never known until that day....

What can this be, this mysterious movement that I speak of here in connection with love only, but which may well take place in the smallest events of life? Is it I know not what sacrifice or inner embrace, is it the profoundest desire to be soul for a soul, or the consciousness, ever quickening within us, of the presence of a life that is invisible, but equal to our own? Is it all that is admirable and sorrowful in the mere act of living that, at such moments, floods our being—is it the aspect of life, one and indivisible? I know not; but in truth it is then that we feel that there lurks, somewhere, an unknown force; it is then that we feel that we are the treasures of an unknown God who loves all, that not a gesture of this God may pass unperceived, and that we are at length in the regions of things that do not betray themselves....

Certain it is that, from the day of our birth to the day of our death, we never emerge from this clearly defined region, but wander in God like helpless sleep-walkers, or like the blind who despairingly seek the very temple in which they do indeed befind themselves. We are there in life, man against man, soul against soul, and day and night are spent under arms. We never see each other, we never touch each other. We see nothing but bucklers and helmets, we touch nothing but iron and brass. But let a tiny circumstance, come from the simpleness of the sky, for one instant only cause the weapons to fall, are there not always tears beneath the helmet, childlike smiles behind the buckler, and is not another verity revealed?

He thought for a moment, then went on, more sadly: A woman—as I believe I told you just now—a woman to whom I had caused suffering against my will—for the most careful of us scatter suffering around them without their knowledge—a woman to whom I had caused suffering against my will, revealed to me one evening the sovereign power of this invisible good. To be good we must needs have suffered; but perhaps it is necessary to have caused suffering before we can become better. This was brought home to me that evening. I felt that I had arrived, alone, at that sad zone of kisses when it seems to us that we are visiting the hovels of the poor, while she, who had lingered on the road, was still smiling in the palace of the first days. Love, as men understand it, was

18

dying between us like a child stricken with a disease come one knows not whence, a disease that has no pity. We said nothing. It would be impossible for me to recall what my thoughts were at that earnest moment. They were doubtless of no significance. I was probably thinking of the last face I had seen, of the quivering gleam of a lantern at a deserted street corner; and, nevertheless, everything took place in a light a thousand times purer, a thousand times higher, than had there intervened all the forces of pity and love which I command in my thoughts and my heart. We parted, and not a word was spoken, but at one and the same moment had we understood our inexpressible thought. We know now that another love had sprung to life, a love that demands not the words, the little attentions and smiles of ordinary love. We have never met again. Perhaps centuries will elapse before we ever do meet again.

"Much is to learn, much to forget,

Through worlds I shall traverse not a few."

before we shall again find ourselves in the same movement of the soul as on that evening: but we can well afford to wait....

And thus, ever since that day, have I greeted, in all places, even in the very bitterest of moments, the beneficent presence of this marvellous power. He who has but once clearly seen it, shall never again find it possible to turn away from its face. You will often behold it smiling in the last retreat of hatred, in the depths of the cruellest tears. And yet does it not reveal itself to the eyes of the body. Its nature changes from the moment that it manifests itself by means of an exterior act; and we are no longer in the truth according to the soul, but in a kind of falsehood as conceived by man. Goodness and love that are self-conscious have no influence on the soul, for they have departed from the kingdoms where they have their dwelling; but, do they only remain blind, they can soften Destiny itself. I have known more than one man who performed every act of kindness and mercy without touching a single soul; and I have known others; who seemed to live in falsehood and injustice, yet were no souls driven from them nor did any for an instant even believe that these men were not good. Nay, more,

19

even those who do not know you, who are merely told of your acts of goodness and deeds of love—if you be not good according to the invisible goodness, these, even, will feel that something is lacking, and they will never be touched in the depths of their being. One might almost believe that there exists, somewhere, a place where all is weighed in the presence of the spirits, or perhaps, out yonder, the other side of the night, a reservoir of certitudes whither the silent herd of souls flock every morning to slake their thirst.

Perhaps we do not yet know what the word "to love" means. There are within us lives in which we love unconsciously. To love thus means more than to have pity, to make inner sacrifices, to be anxious to help and give happiness; it is a thing that lies a thousand fathoms deeper, where our softest, swiftest, strongest words cannot reach it. At moments we might believe it to be a recollection, furtive, but excessively keen, of the great primitive unity. There is in this love a force that nothing can resist. Which of us—and he question himself the side of the light, from which our gaze is habitually averted—which of us but will find in himself the recollection of certain strange workings of this force? Which of us, when by the side of the most ordinary person perhaps, but has suddenly become conscious of the advent of something that none had summoned? Was it the soul, or perhaps life, that had turned within itself like a sleeper on the point of awakening? I know not; nor did you know, and no one spoke of it; but you did not separate from each other as though nothing had happened.

To love thus is to love according to the soul; and there is no soul that does not respond to this love. For the soul of man is a guest that has gone hungry these centuries back, and never has it to be summoned twice to the nuptial feast.

The souls of all our brethren are ever hovering about us, craving for a caress, and only waiting for the signal. But how many beings there are who all their life long have not dared make such a signal!

It is the disaster of our entire existence that we live thus away from our soul, and stand in such dread of its slightest movement. Did we but allow it to smile frankly in its silence and its radiance, we

20

should be already living an eternal life. We have only to think for an instant how much it succeeds in accomplishing during those rare moments when we knock off its chains—for it is our custom to enchain it as though it were distraught—what it does in love, for instance, for there we do permit it at times to approach the lattices of external life. And would it not be in accordance with the primal truth if all men were to feel that they were face to face with each other, even as the woman feels with the man she loves?

This invisible and divine goodness, of which I only speak here because of its being one of the surest and nearest signs of the unceasing activity of our soul, this invisible and divine goodness ennobles, in decisive fashion, all that it has unconsciously touched. Let him who has a grievance against his fellow, descend into himself and seek out whether he never has been good in the presence of that fellow.

For myself, I have never met any one by whose side I have felt my invisible goodness bestir itself, without he has become, at that very instant, better than myself. Be good at the depths of you, and you will discover that those who surround you will be good even to the same depths.

Nothing responds more infallibly to the secret cry of goodness than the secret cry of goodness that is near.

While you are actively good in the invisible, all those who approach you will unconsciously do things that they could not do by the side of any other man.

Therein lies a force that has no name; a spiritual rivalry that knows no resistance. It is as though this were the actual place where is the sensitive spot of our soul; for there are souls that seem to have forgotten their existence and to have renounced everything that enables the being to rise; but, once touched here, they all draw themselves erect; and in the divine plains of the secret goodness, the most humble of souls cannot endure defeat.

And yet it is possible that nothing is changing in the life one sees; but is it only that which matters, and is our existence indeed confined to actions we can take in our hand like stones on the highroad? If you ask yourself, as we are told we should ask every evening, "what of immortal have I done to-day?" Is it always on the material side that we can count, weigh and measure unerringly; is it there that you must begin your search? It is possible for you to cause extraordinary tears to flow; it is possible that you may fill a heart with unheard-of certitudes, and give eternal life unto a soul, and no one shall know of it, nor shall you even know yourself. It may be that nothing is changing; it may be that were it put to the test all would crumble, and that this goodness we speak of would yield to the smallest fear. It matters not. Something divine has happened; and somewhere must our God have smiled.

May it not be the supreme aim of life thus to bring to birth the inexplicable within ourselves; and do we know how much we add to ourselves when we awake something of the incomprehensible that slumbers in every corner? Here you have awakened love which will not fall asleep again. The soul that your soul has regarded, that has wept with you the holy tears of the solemn joy that none may behold, will bear you no resentment, not even in the midst of torture. It will not even feel the need of forgiving. So convinced is it of one knows not what, that nothing can henceforth dim or efface the smile that it wears within; for nothing can ever separate two souls which, for an instant, "have been good together."

SILENCE

As we advance through life, it is more and more brought home to us that nothing takes place that is not in accord with some curious, preconceived design: and of this we never breathe a word, we scarcely dare to let our minds dwell upon it, but of its existence, somewhere above our heads, we are absolutely convinced. The most fatuous of men smiles, at the first encounters, as though he were the accomplice of the destiny of his brethren. And in this domain, even those who can speak the most profoundly realise— they, perhaps, more than others—that words can never express the real, special relationship that exists between two beings.

Were I to speak to you at this moment of the gravest things of all— of love, death or destiny—it is not love, death or destiny that I should touch; and, my efforts notwithstanding, there would always remain between us a truth which had not been spoken, which we had not even thought of speaking; and yet it is this truth only, voiceless though it has been, which will have lived with us for an instant, and by which we shall have been wholly absorbed. For that truth, was our truth as regards death, destiny or love, and it was in silence only that we could perceive it. And nothing save only the silence will have had any importance. "My sisters," says a child in the fairy-story, "you have each of you a secret thought—I wish to know it." We, too, have something that people wish to know, but it is hidden far above the secret thought—it is our secret silence.

But all questions are useless. When our spirit is alarmed, its own agitation becomes a barrier to the second life that lives in this secret; and, would we know what it is that lies hidden there, we must cultivate silence among ourselves, for it is then only that for one instant the eternal flowers unfold their petals, the mysterious flowers whose form and colour are ever changing in harmony with the soul that is by their side. As gold and silver are weighed in pure water, so does the soul test its weight in silence, and the words that we let fall have no meaning apart from the silence that wraps them round. If I tell someone that I love him—as I may have told a hundred others—my words will convey nothing to him; but the silence which will ensue, if I do indeed love him, will make clear in what depths lie the roots of my love, and will in its turn give birth to a conviction, that shall itself be silent; and in the course of a lifetime, this silence and this conviction will never again be the same....

Is it not silence that determines and fixes the savour of love? Deprived of it, love would lose its eternal essence and perfume. Who has not known those silent moments which separated the lips to reunite the souls? It is these that we must ever seek. There is no silence more docile than the silence of love, and it is indeed the only one that we may claim for ourselves alone. The other great silences, those of death, grief or destiny, do not belong to us. They come towards us at their own hour, following in the track of events, and those whom they do not meet need not reproach themselves. But we can all go forth to meet the silence of love. They lie in wait for us, night and day, at our threshold, and are no less beautiful than their brothers. And it is thanks to them that those who have seldom wept may know the life of the soul almost as intimately as those to whom much grief has come: and therefore it is that such of us as have loved deeply have learnt many secrets that are unknown to others: for thousands and thousands of things quiver in silence on the lips of true friendship and love, that are not to be found in the silence of other lips, to which friendship and love are unknown....

CPSIA information can be obtained
at www.ICGtesting.com
Printed in the USA
BVHW050905240423
662927BV00013B/953

9 781517 174873